Preface: The Princess & Dragon Story

This collection of stories has a very special meaning. It takes me back to the early days of being a father with a beautiful little girl sitting on my knee for story time.

Like all little girls, she loved stories about princesses and dragons. She still does! This volume is dedicated to her.

Of course, this collection isn't just for girls! There are plenty of dragons, knights and other adventures that boys will love. I know first-hand because my boys (6 and 10) loved reading every story before they were published.

It seems there is nothing more treasured in literature than the princess and dragon story. Why? Because children love adventure and danger, heroes and heroines, and of course, happy endings. Every story, every word, every adventure, every daring rescue, every lesson learned — it's all new and exciting to children.

Through these stories, they explore the world around them. They learn about good vs. evil, about friendship and love, about right and wrong, about choices and consequences and so much more.

And all the while, their inquisitive minds are learning new vocabulary, improving listening and reading skills, and literally being hard-wired to learn

- preparing them to become successful in school and

in life.

There is no better early childhood development

program than when a parent takes the time to sit

down and read with a child every day. To that end,

we offer you this special collection of timeless

princess and dragon stories in the hope that both you

and your child will love the experience of joining in

the adventures and excitement together.

Phillip J. Chipping // Founder
knowonder! publishing
www.knowonder.com

About DyslexiAssist™

Part of our mission at Knowonder! Publishing is to make literacy more effective. In order to fulfill that mission for children suffering from dyslexia we are proud to announce our new DyslexiAssist™ initiative: to publish each of our books in a special font designed to make reading easier for dyslexics. You can learn more about it on our website at:

www.knowonder.com/dyslexiassist

When reading with this new font, independent research shows that 84% of dyslexics read faster, 77% read with fewer mistakes, and 76% recommend the font to others who suffer from dyslexia.

But the magic isn't just in the font. We take

extra care to make the font an appropriate size, give

proper spacing to letters in the words, make sure that

there are the exact right number of words on each

line, and so much more! The layout of the book is just

as important. We go to extra lengths to make sure

all the stars are aligned so they, too, can know the

wonder of reading.

Reading stories is a highly enjoyable form of

entertainment but people with dyslexia have been

unable to find the same joy from books. We hope this

new initiative can now bring the same love and joy of

reading and learning to your home!

Table of Contents

A collection

of princess and dragon stories

(perfect for bedtime!)

for children ages 0-12

and for parents

who want to feel like a kid again.

- Volume 4 -

Stock photography and artwork from
istockphoto.com or dreamstime.com, unless otherwise noted.

ISBN: 978-15303191-8-3

Dedicated to my princess,
my "darling angel baby doll."
I love you forever!

A Dragon on the High Hill

by David Turnbull

When Pa came in through the cottage door, Wil

looked up from the messy scribble that was his

homework. Pa hung his coat on the hook and took a

seat by the fire.

"They're finally going to do something about that

dragon up on the High Hill," he said.

"About time too," said Ma, stirring the broth that

was bubbling away on the range.

A log burning on the fire sent a cinder hissing onto

the hearth. Pa reached across and stubbed it out

with the tip of his shepherd's crook.

"What are they going to do?" asked Wil.

Normally dragons lived to the north, where the Far

Tundra met the Serrated Mountains, but this one had

ended up in Low Counties and had made its lair up

on crags of the High Hill. It had been a nuisance for

months now, scorching crops in the fields, damaging

church spires and, worst of all, leaving huge mounds

of dragon dung piled up everywhere.

Wil had actually seen a mound of dragon dung

in his neighbor's back yard. Remembering the awful

stench of it he screwed up his nose.

"There was a big meeting," Pa told him. "All the

mayors from all the villages across all of the Low

Counties."

Wil pushed his homework to one side. "They decided what to do about the dragon?"

"Eventually," replied Pa. "None of them have ever dealt with a dragon crisis before. But from what I heard they agreed straight off that fetching a dragon slayer from Tennanbrau City would be too expensive."

"Quite right too," agreed Ma, setting the soup bowls out on the table. "We pay enough taxes as it is."

Wil didn't like the idea of a dragon slayer. The dragon might be a pest, but that was no reason for someone to go after it with a lance or a blunderbuss.

"Laying traps in the fields was another

suggestion," said Pa. "But then it was pointed out that sheep might wander into them."

"And what about the children?" added Ma. "What if Wil accidentally stepped on one?"

Wil smirked to himself. He had his wits about him. He wasn't likely to go stepping on a dragon trap.

But Pa agreed with Ma.

"It would have been negligent to say the least," he said. "So the mayors argued all through the night. For every suggesting there were at least two arguments against." He stretched out his legs and warmed his socks in front of the fire. "Eventually they concluded their only real option was to send a team of hunters up to the High Hill with their dogs."

"That'll cost money too," said Ma. She ladled the broth into the soup bowls and beckoned them both to the table.

"Not as much as a professional dragon slayer." Pa took his seat and tore off a hunk of bread from the freshly baked loaf that Ma had set down earlier. "I said they could use our old barn as a base."

Ma placed the soup pot back on the range and swung round. Her face was red. "You did what?"

"I said they could use our old barn," repeated Pa. "Our farm is the nearest to the foot of the High Hill."

"I hope they're not expecting to be fed," said Ma.

"They'll bring cheese and biscuits for their

breakfast," Pa assured her.

Wil lifted up a spoonful of his broth and blew on it to cool it down.

"When are they coming?" asked Ma. She looked even more flustered.

"This evening," replied Pa. "They want to make a start at first light."

Ma wiped her hands on her apron. "They can't come this evening. The place is a mess. I haven't had time to tidy up. Wil, you'll have to help me."

"They're only going to use the old barn," laughed Pa. "They're not coming to the house."

"Well I hope not," said Ma, finally taking her seat. "I don't want people gossiping in the village that the Redcap's keep an untidy house."

Wil swallowed down a mouthful of broth. Turning to Pa, he asked the question that had been churning in his mind since the first mention of the hunters. "When they go up to the High Hill can I go with them? I'd like to see them catch the dragon."

"Certainly not!" cried Ma. "It's too dangerous. You'd get yourself burned to a crisp."

"Besides," said Pa. "They're not going to catch the dragon. They're going to kill it."

Later that evening Wil snuck around the side of the old barn. Ma was reading her book by the fireside while Pa sharpened the blades of his big scissors on the whetstone, getting them ready for the sheep-shearing season. Both of them thought Wil was in his room finishing his homework.

Half an hour earlier he had watched the red-bearded hunters arrive, their crossbows slung over their burly shoulders and their dogs straining against their leashes. Now he desperately wanted to listen in on what they were planning.

Through a space in the wooden slats of the old barn Wil could see the dogs lying down in a group just beyond where the hunters sat on a pile of old wool sacks, bathed in the flickering glow from their night lamps. They were talking about what trophies they would take once they killed the dragon.

"I'll have the wings," said one. "I know a man who

makes excellent umbrellas."

"I'll take the skin," said another. "It'll make a fine leather jerkin for the winter."

The third hunter rose to his feet. He took up his crossbow and loaded a bolt. Wil felt his heart quicken. Did they know he was there spying on them?

The hunter shouldered the crossbow and took aim at something at the far end of the barn. Squinting his eyes, Wil could just make out they had chalked a crude outline of a dragon on the far wall of the barn.

The hunter released his bolt with a loud thump. The three men let out a boisterous cheer that set the dogs off barking. Wil saw that the bolt had hit the chalk dragon right in the middle of its head.

"I'll take its teeth," said the hunter, over the racket of the dogs. "My wife wants a necklace for our anniversary."

That's horrible, thought Wil, hurrying back across the yard. I'm going to have to find a way to save the dragon.

Next morning, while it was still quite dark, Wil climbed out of his bedroom window. He followed the winding path that led through the bracken and the heather and up to the steep slope of the High Hill. By the time the red glow of the sun was peeping over the summit, he had already reached the area where the path became nothing but loose rock and shale.

The wind gusted all around him. It was so strong

he had to bend his head into it when he walked.

Although he looked all around for a cave that might

be big enough for a dragon to make its lair, he

couldn't see anything. Down below, the hunters were

already passing along the heather path with their

dogs galloping ahead of them.

He was running out of time.

In a panic he rushed around, looking here and

there. He kept slipping on the shale and falling down.

Although the hunters were still quite some way down,

he could hear the barking of the dogs carried up to

the High Hill by the gushing wind. Then, in the rays

of the rising sun, he saw a fleeting dark shadow

streak across the rocks.

The dragon?

Wil looked up, and there she was, circling in the sky right above his head.

She swooped lower and lower with each circuit, powerful wings rising and falling. The hunters must have seen her too, because he heard their excited shouts as the barking of their dogs grew louder and more aggressive.

The dragon glided in low, almost skimming the jagged rocks, wings stretched wide and hind legs curled up at her sides. She flew right over Wil's head, and the powerful downdraft knocked him down onto his back. He watched in amazement as her yellow underbelly passed swiftly over him. Quickly he rolled over in time to see her dive down behind a craggy outcropping.

There's a cave behind there, thought Wil. The entrance is hidden. That's why I couldn't see it.

He scrambled to his feet and ran up the slope.

The hunters were gaining fast. But Wil was far better at running than he ever was at homework. He pushed himself onwards, slipping and skidding on the grey shale.

When he reached the outcrop he hauled himself up, arms straining. The wind went gusting about him as if it was trying to blow him clean off the High Hill. Scrapping his knees and his hands as he went, he tumbled down the other side.

And there, right in front of him, instead of the concealed entrance to a cave, stood the dragon.

Large as life — ridged humps on her back, green scales on her hoary hide, wings folded neatly in at her sides. Growling menacingly, she turned to face him and bared her needle-sharp teeth.

As Wil jumped to his feet, her nostrils flared and puffs of white smoke billowed out. With a roar she lashed out with her barbed tail, sending tiny glistening shards of rock tumbling into the air.

He should have been afraid — but all he could think was how beautiful the dragon looked.

She drew a mighty breath and ran straight at him. He could hear the sharp clicking of the little stone organs in her throat striking together to make

the spark that would ignite the fiery gas from her

lungs. He realized how foolhardy he'd been. Any

minute now he was going to be engulfed in a ball of

flaming breath and burned to a crisp just as Ma had

predicted.

Then he remembered what his Pa had told him to

do if one of the rams ever charged at him when he

was out tending the sheep. Every Low County father

told his son or daughter the same thing—smack it

hard on the snout!

Instead of trying to dodge out of the way of the

dragon, Wil ran to meet her. He could see she was

getting ready to breathe out. He raised his hand

high, and as soon as he got close enough, he brought it down sharply onto the dragon's gleaming black muzzle. A loud smack echoed off the rocks.

The dragon let out a howl of pain. A thick blast of hot air knocked Wil from his feet. Although the breath had not ignited in the back of her throat, Wil was still left dazed from the impact. Keening noisily, the dragon took flight, her wings tossing up eruptions of rock dust all around.

The hunters were already up on top of the craggy outcrop. Their dogs raced past Wil, snapping at the departing heels of the dragon. Two of the men fired off bolts from their crossbows. But the dragon was too fast for them. Up and up she went until she was just a green spec in the blue ocean of the sky.

"You'll be in big trouble if she comes back," warned one of the dragon hunters as they all crowded angrily around Wil.

Suddenly the dragon swooped back down at a terrifying speed. The dragon hunters were so surprised, they dove for cover. Wil stood his ground; somehow he knew that she wasn't going to hurt him.

Hovering for a magnificent moment only a foot or two above him, the dragon dropped something from inside her mouth. Wil caught the object—a precious gemstone from the cave where she had made her lair—a gift for his selfless act in saving her life. Turning the glistening stone over in his hand, he watched as she rose once more and disappeared with

her mighty wings unfurled into the misty swirl of a

cloud.

"She won't be back," Wil told the dazed dragon

hunters. Then smiling proudly, he popped the dragon's

gift into his pocket.

the end.

The Golden Hamster

by Shari L. Klase

Long ago and many kingdoms away lived a lovely

young princess. Her name was Isodore. She was

pampered and petted by all who knew her, particularly

by her father, King Feodore. She was, therefore,

spoiled and selfish. Her mother had died when she

was a baby, and so her father would do anything for

her.

Her room was a tower of the palace at the edge

of the kingdom surrounded by woods, and she liked

nothing better than playing in her gardens, except

for one thing. She was afraid of the birds that

flew there. Her fear was so intense her father had

enclosed her personal gardens in golden wire so as to

keep out the many birds that frequented there to eat

the seeds. Isodore forbid anyone to feed the birds, so

no bird feeders cheered the pleasant gardens.

However, for all that, she had a soft spot for one

palace pet, a little golden hamster named Henry she

kept in a silver cage in her room. For that one she

kept seeds that would have fed many a bird had she

not despised them so.

Her hostility toward birds began innocently enough.

When she was a toddler of about two or three, there

had been many birds in the palace gardens. She had

found them as fascinating as any child would have.

One day, she saw a tiny blue jay on the grass ahead

of her. Excited and squealing with joy, she dashed to

it. Just as she was ready to scoop it up, a flutter of

wings sprang upon her head and claws attacked her.

Anger and fear replaced her joy as she screamed with terror and rage. No amount of pleading by her nurse could soothe her. "The bird was only defending her baby," she reassured her.

But small ears wouldn't listen. From that moment on, Isodore disliked birds and the entire palace must dislike them with her.

But she didn't despise her golden hamster. She delighted in the way he sat up and begged for seeds, his eager, bright eyes stared inquisitively at her. Most of all, he loved sunflower seeds. She gave them to Henry every night. Each one he took with delight and stuffed into his cheek pouches. Oddly enough, she had never seen him eat even one sunflower seed, though he ate voraciously of other seeds in his dish, and she could see no shells in his cage as telltale signs of eating them at a more private hour.

Then one night the Princess discovered his secret. She had trouble sleeping that night. Bad dreams of birds flapping about her plagued her. Waking, she turned to her pampered pet. However, with a wave of shock, she realized he wasn't there. She searched the hiding places in his cage, but there was no golden hamster anywhere. Alarmed, she awakened her entire staff and had them search everywhere in the palace. The search was fruitless. They could not discover his whereabouts.

"My child, it is useless." Her father patted her. "But surely, he will turn up in time."

Tears glistened in her eyes and she wailed. "But Henry may be carelessly killed by the maids, thinking him a mouse."

Her father hugged her. "Have some care for the servants as you care for this creature. They have been searching for hours. I will alert the maids to be careful of what they kill in the kitchen."

The young princess went back to her chambers, but she could not sleep. The little hamster was her only concern, but as daylight dawned, her eyes grew heavy. Then she saw a tiny, fleeting figure. It scurried up to its cage, squeezed its fat, little body through the bars, and popped itself into the cage. Startled, Isodore gasped. Then she clasped her hands in joy and shouted.

"Oh Henry, you naughty little hamster, you had me worried so!"

She scooped him up, nuzzled him to her face, and forgave him. However, as the day grew to night, she began to wonder if Henry ever repeated his escapades. So she remained awake in her bed that night. Sure enough the little hamster did not disappoint her. He squeezed his head between his bars, popped his fluffy body out, and scurried away.

She did not awaken the staff this time but waited quietly in her bed, dozing only briefly. Sure enough he returned bright-eyed and content again to be her

captive pet.

"Ah, he is only looking for adventure," she

thought.

She informed her father. He smiled. "A little

explorer," he commented. "I wonder where he goes?

He had better be careful of the palace cat."

The princess cried out in dismay. She had not

thought of that. Besides, she did wonder where his

journey led. So she decided to find out.

As he began his venture, she silently followed him.

The Princess could be as quiet as a cat, and that

night she was. She imagined herself stalking her little

friend and smiled. Out the palace he scampered and

into the palace garden, right into the very heart of the garden with the golden fence surrounding it. She sank into the flowers and watched as Henry sat up upon his haunches and sniffed the air.

"What is he searching for?" she wondered. But sooner than she could wonder longer about this, out hopped a sight that filled her with horror. It was a wounded bird, yes, but worst of all, a blue jay! Obviously, it was unable to fly. It approached the hamster, and before Isodore could cry out, Henry popped out each and every one of his sunflower seeds from his cheek pouches. He lovingly placed them before the bird. The bird quickly gobbled them down.

The Princess was horrified! She turned and ran

quietly back to the palace. Henry, her best friend, was a traitor. He was helping the thing she detested most in the world. Hot tears of anger washed down her cheeks. Yet, she could not stay mad at him for long. He was her beloved pet. One could not choose whom to love. She could not help but love Henry, and Henry could not help but love the bird.

For a few nights, she followed him and always he repeated his nightly feedings. She began to feel a twinge of pity for the flightless bird. In the morning, she would stroke Henry fondly.

"So you love another," she would say and chuckle a bit.

But the more she thought about Henry and his

mission to feed the bird, the more she began to

worry. After all, as her father had said, there was

the palace cat. Henry was taking chances sneaking

around palace corridors while the cat was on duty.

Yet, she knew, Henry considered it his duty to

take care of the helpless bird. Isodore was feeling

something she had never felt before, pity for someone

she had formerly detested.

"Perhaps the best solution is for me to feed

the bird myself," she said, but she trembled at the

thought. Would she really be able to confront her

fear? She didn't know. But for Henry's sake, she

must try.

Isodore put feet to her resolve the very next night.

She filled her pockets with sunflower seeds. Instead of going right to sleep, she removed Henry from the cage and carried him to her own little garden. Then she placed him gently on the ground. Henry seemed a bit surprised by the method of transportation to his usual spot. As Henry watched with curiosity, Isodore removed the seeds from her pockets and tossed them on the ground. Then she hid in the bushes nearby.

The bird crept out from its hiding place, stepped forward, picked up a seed and began to eat. Isodore turned away in fear and was about to make her escape when she heard a voice.

"Wait!" it said.

She gasped and turned. The form of the bird had

changed. Standing in its place was a prince. Even more astounding, standing in Henry's place was a prince's squire.

"Thank you, Princess, I was growing quite tired of eating seeds and living in a cage," Henry said, laughing.

"Yes, thank you," the prince said. "I am Prince Jay. I and my servant were under a spell for these years. I had been selfish and heartless in my youth. Because you were much like me, you were chosen as my salvation. However, only when you could show me pity out of your own hands, would I and my squire be released. I was doomed to live until then as your enemy, and my squire was to live as your beloved pet.

Henry befriended you so he could help me."

Isodore smiled at him and took his hand. "You are not my enemy now," she said.

"I thought you detested birds," he said softly.

"No, my best friend taught me to love one. You know, you cannot choose whom to love. Life chooses for you."

"Yes," he smiled. "That is so."

As you know, and do not doubt it, they lived happily ever after as little larks.

the end.

Finding the Perfect Job for a Dragon

by Elizabeth Glann

The rain had ended during the night and only

sparkling droplets remained on flowers and leaves

in the garden. Barefooted, Miranda danced out the

door, eager to step in the nearby puddles. But before

she could even dip in one toe, she saw something

that made her stop. Underneath a small bush,

something was moving.

Miranda squatted down to get a better look. Two

bright eyes belonging to a tiny green animal stared

out at her. Miranda held her breath. Then she gently

reached into the bush until she could touch the little

creature's scales. The animal didn't move. After

another minute had passed, Miranda was able to lift

it out. It was wet and shivering, and Miranda hurried

inside the house.

"What are you holding?" her mother asked.

"It looks like a baby dragon," Miranda answered.

"It needs someone to take care of it." She wrapped a

towel around the little green animal, and it closed its

eyes and seemed to be smiling.

"A dragon!" Miranda's mother said. "We can't keep a dragon in the house."

"Please," Miranda begged. "I'll take care of it. You won't even know it's here."

Her mother looked down at the little creature. "Well, it is kind of cute," she said. "It's no bigger than a mouse. Do you promise to take care of it?"

Miranda nodded.

"All right," her mother said. "We'll see how it goes."

Miranda clapped her hands. "I'm going to name him Huffy." She made a bed out of a shoe box for her new pet, and Huffy slept beside Miranda's bed that night.

At first he was satisfied with scraps from the table, but soon he had to have his own plate of food at each meal. Then even that wasn't enough. Miranda had to find a bigger box for his bed, and still he continued to grow and GROW. At last she couldn't find any box big enough, and Huffy just slept at the foot of her bed. On winter nights, his hot breath kept her feet warm.

But one day Miranda's mother said, "Huffy is eating us out of house and home. We can't afford to keep him any longer unless he finds a job and earns a paycheck to help out."

When Huffy heard the news, he looked worried.

"I'd be glad to work," he said, "but what jobs can a dragon do?"

Miranda handed Huffy the employment ads from the newspaper, and Huffy read each one carefully, circling anything that looked promising.

Miranda's father offered to loan Huffy a shirt and tie, and at last Huffy was ready for his first interview.

"How do I look?" he asked Miranda anxiously.

"You look so handsome I should call you Sir Huffy," she answered.

Huffy trudged from one circled job to the next, but no one seemed to want to hire a dragon. Finally he reached the last job on his list. It was in an ice cream shop, and the "Help Wanted" ad described it

as "the best job in town."

The boss seemed surprised to see a dragon, but he

agreed to talk to Huffy.

"You look strong, but can you stand on your feet

all day and still be pleasant to the customers?" he

asked.

"That won't be hard," Huffy answered. "I like

people."

"Then you're hired," the boss said. "One more

thing I think you'll like. You can have a heaping bowl

of ice cream every day. Free!"

"Hooray!" Huffy shouted. "This is the best job in

town."

Miranda was thrilled to learn that Huffy had found

work. She grabbed one of his front paws, and around

the room they whirled in a happy dance.

On his first day of work, Miranda went to the

ice cream parlor with her pet. The shop looked just

like Huffy had described. The walls were covered in

white tile, and each of the red seats at the counter

could spin in either direction. Miranda took one of the

red seats and waited for Huffy. Soon he appeared,

wearing the white coat the boss had given him. He

asked Miranda what she wanted to eat.

"First order coming up," he called as he began

to dish up an ice cream sundae. But before he could

even place a cherry on top, disaster struck. Huffy's

hot breath melted all the ice cream, and the boss

yelled, "You're fired!"

Huffy left the shop in tears. "I didn't even get to

eat a free bowl of ice cream," he said sadly.

Miranda did her best to cheer him up. "That job

just wasn't right for you," she said. "I know you'll

find a better one."

As soon as they got home, they heard about

another opportunity for Huffy. The children who lived

next door loved the dragon, and their parents were

looking for a baby-sitter.

Huffy was excited when he was offered the job. "I

know I'll like this work," he said. "I always have fun

playing with the kids."

"I'm sure you'll be good at this, Huffy," Miranda agreed.

At first the job went well. Huffy read stories to the kids and played with them. But after a while the kids wanted to go outside. Then the trouble started.

When the kids started to climb the ladder, Huffy moved to the foot of the slide to catch them. All of a sudden he heard little Bobby yell, "Ow! It's too hot!"

Huffy suggested the kids move to the see-saw, but the same thing happened. "I can't sit on this," Susie cried. "It feels like it's on fire!"

Just then the parents arrived home, and Huffy lost another job.

"But we really like Huffy," the children wailed,

and along with Huffy, they too had tears in their eyes

as they waved good-bye.

This time Huffy felt really sad. "I didn't mean

to make everything so hot," he said. "I can't stop

breathing. I'll never be able to find a job I'm good

at."

Miranda didn't know what to do to make Huffy

feel better. At last she said, "Let's go to a movie.

We'll find a happy one. That's sure to cheer you up."

They bought their tickets and went inside the

theater.

"How about some popcorn, Huffy?" Miranda asked,

but then she noticed the line that stretched all the

way around the lobby.

"Waiting in line will take too long," Huffy answered sadly. Suddenly his eyes lit up. "I think there is something I can do to help."

Miranda watched as he made his way to the manager's office.

When she saw him a few minutes later, he wore a white apron. He waved at her but didn't stop to talk. Instead he walked quickly to the popcorn wagon and puffed on the unpopped kernels of corn. In just a minute or two, the lobby smelled like hot, buttery popcorn. Everyone standing in line cheered.

The manager hired Huffy on the spot.

When Miranda went to the afternoon show

yesterday, she saw a plaque hanging over the popcorn

wagon.

"Employee of the Month,

Huffy the Dragon."

"You were right, Miranda," Huffy said when he

took his break. "I finally found a great job. The best

part is it's one that only I can do."

Then he turned his attention once more to the

task of making popcorn which is, after all, the perfect

job for a dragon.

the end.

Princess Poppy and the Little Dragon

by Rosemary Gemmell

Princess Poppy was tired of being a pretty little girl with long curly hair and frilly dresses. Her big brother, Prince Percival, attended sword fencing classes. Percival and his friends also learned how to shoot a bow and arrow.

"Why can't I learn to fight?" Princess Poppy asked every day.

"You're only a little girl. You can't fight dragons and ogres," Percival said.

Poppy hid behind a tree and watched the boys pretending to fight dangerous dragons.

"Take that!" Percival shouted as he lunged forward with his short sword and pierced the sack hanging from a hook.

Poppy didn't think much of the boys' fighting skills.

A fire-breathing dragon wasn't likely to stand still.

They wouldn't get close enough to use the sword, and

they couldn't shoot the arrows far enough. She tried

to tell her brother.

"Your small arrow won't harm a thick-skinned

dragon," Poppy said.

"What do you know about it?" Percival answered.

"Girls don't know how to fight dragons and you're a

princess. You need strong boys to protect you. Like

me and my friends."

Poppy laughed at them and walked away. She knew

more about animals and magical creatures than any of

the boys. She liked reading the books in the palace

library and knew about the kind of herbs and plants to heal wounds. But Percival thought books were boring.

One day, a knight rode into the palace courtyard and called for the king. Poppy listened as the knight told her father about the fierce dragon in the next village.

"Has the dragon killed many people?" the king asked.

The knight rubbed his nose. "Well, no, Your Majesty, although the dragon is big and fierce."

The king frowned. "You mean none of the knights has tried to kill it yet? What's wrong with you?"

Poppy watched the knight kneel in front of her

father. "If you please, Your Majesty, most of the knights are away fighting a war in another land."

The king sighed. "You're all useless. Even my son and his friends are braver than you. Go and find me some men brave enough to tackle the dragon."

Poppy stood still until the king dismissed the knight, then she crept up to her brother's room. She would show them how to catch a dragon. She found Percival's sword under the bed while he was at his counting lessons. Poppy lifted it up, surprised to find it quite heavy. She borrowed her brother's spare tunic and thick tights and hurried back to her room.

Standing in front of the mirror, Poppy fastened a strong belt around her waist and stuck the short sword through it. Then she tied her long hair up and covered it with a hat before pushing her feet into her sturdiest shoes. She was ready to go hunting. Before leaving, she remembered to put some of her best healing ointment into a little bag tied to her belt.

Poppy crept away from the palace, hoping no one would guess she was the palace princess. Soon she was on the green hillside. Her legs felt lighter in the tights with no silly dress tripping her up. This was fun! She forgot about dragons and ran over the hills and through the glens until she heard groaning and moaning coming from behind the next hill.

Making sure the sword was ready to pull from her belt, Poppy crept forward to see what caused such a noise. As she reached the top of the hill, she took a deep breath then peeped over the edge.

A small dragon lay on the ground, moving its big head from side to side while groaning and growling.

"Waaaargh! Grrrrrwl!"

Poppy had never heard a sound like it. She watched, expecting to see a blast of fiery breath. But none came. She frowned. What was wrong and why didn't it fly away?

Suddenly, the little dragon turned its head in her direction and looked straight at her with big almond-shaped eyes. Poppy gulped. Now its fiery breath would appear.

The dragon tried to stand but kept falling back

onto the ground. Very strange, Poppy decided. The dragon looked fierce with its scaly body, big head, and long snout, and she could see those large teeth when it groaned. But even though it had two small wings, it made no attempt to fly away.

The moaning and groaning got louder as the dragon stared at Poppy again. Maybe she was imagining it, but the dragon's eyes seemed to be pleading with her, as though it tried to tell her something.

Poppy grasped her sword in one hand and edged toward the dragon. Since it was only a little one and she hadn't seen any fire, surely it wouldn't hurt her? Swallowing the lump in her dry throat, she took another step closer.

The little dragon continued to moan. Soon, Poppy almost reached its side. Then she noticed what was wrong. One of the dragon's feet was caught in a horrible trap.

Poppy gasped. No wonder the poor little dragon seemed in pain and couldn't fly away. Could she help? Poppy crept up close to the dragon and whispered softly to it.

"Don't worry, little dragon, I'll set you free. But you must stay still. I won't hurt you."

At the sound of her voice, the dragon stopped groaning and listened, as though it understood. Poppy kept whispering while she bent down to see how to free it. The trap's iron teeth had snapped shut to grip the foot. Poppy thought for a moment. She pulled

out the sword. The short blade looked sturdy enough.

Pushing the tip of the sword into the trap, and

careful not to touch the dragon's foot, she twisted

the blade this way and that. The trap was stuck fast.

"Waaaargh!" the dragon moaned again. Poppy

nearly fell over.

"Stay still, little dragon," she soothed. Using

both hands, Poppy pushed the sword between the iron

teeth and pulled with all her might. Suddenly, she fell

back. Maybe the sword had broken!

She looked at the trap to find it edged apart.

Careful not to get her hands near the iron teeth,

Poppy pulled at the trap with her sword. The dragon

moved. Poppy stopped. The foot was loose enough to get free.

While she kept the sword in place, little dragon dragged its foot away until clear of the trap. Poppy removed the sword. "Snaaap!" The trap sprang shut again. But little dragon was free, although it had lost a few of its scales. It still seemed in pain, so poppy knelt beside it and opened the small bag attached to her belt. Her pot of herbal ointment was good for cuts. Maybe it would help the dragon's foot.

She put some ointment on her fingers and started talking to the dragon again. "I'm just going to rub a little of this good ointment on your foot. I promise it will help." The dragon listened and watched.

Very gently, Poppy smeared some ointment on little

dragon's cut. The dragon softly moaned but didn't

pull away.

"That's good. Nearly finished," Poppy said, in the

kind of voice the royal nurse used when Poppy hurt

herself.

Poppy sat back on her heels. "There, all done."

She had done everything she could to help. She put

the ointment back in her bag and for good luck, she

added the dragon scales lying on the grass. And now

she'd better hurry away in case little dragon turned

on her now that it was free.

As she stood up, Poppy heard a huge "whooshing"

sound and looked up toward the hill. A very large

dragon with green and black scaly skin stared back.

It opened its huge mouth and a long lick of red and

yellow fire shot out.

Poppy was about to run when she felt something

touch her leg. She looked down to find little dragon's

head resting against her and a soft little "turuck,

turuck" sound coming from it. Little dragon was

trying to thank her!

"What about your father?" Poppy asked. "Or is

that your mother or maybe your big brother?" Poppy

gently moved away from the little dragon, keeping one

eye on the large dragon on the hill. But little dragon

started to follow her!

Now what could she do? As Poppy stood still, the

large dragon inched closer. But it didn't breathe out

any more fire. And suddenly, it bent its front legs

and knelt on the ground. Poppy stared in amazement

as little dragon joined its parent on the hill. The big

dragon kept looking at Poppy. Did it want her to do

something? Why was it kneeling before her?

A strange idea entered Poppy's head as the

two dragons continued to stare. As if she could

understand them, Poppy approached the big dragon.

Still looking at Poppy with gentle eyes, the dragon's

huge wings began to flap slightly, and Poppy knew

what to do.

Pushing the sword into her belt, Poppy climbed

onto the scaly back of the big dragon. Slipping and

sliding a bit, she felt the little dragon push her gently into place with its snout. Gripping the dragon's neck, Poppy waited. Then very slowly, the big dragon spread its wings and gently ran over the hillside until it took flight. Poppy gripped even tighter and closed her eyes. Then she heard a whooshing sound and opened her eyes to see little dragon flying beside her.

Poppy enjoyed the ride. "Whee!" she cried, and laughed as she flew through the air on the back of a dragon. "Turuck!" cried little dragon beside her. Over the hills and under the wide blue sky they flew until Poppy saw her father's palace come into view. The big dragon was taking her home.

Down on the ground, she saw tiny figures running

out from the palace. And as the dragon flew a little lower, she spied her brother and his friends shouting and pointing, swords ready in their hands. Poppy waved and hoped the dragons wouldn't get too close to the palace in case the knights had returned. But the large dragon slowed down and glided gently to a halt behind one of the hills.

As Poppy climbed down, she heard voices in the distance. "Who has mastered the dragon? What manner of knight is he?"

Poppy smiled. She'd forgotten she was dressed in her brother's clothes. But she was worried about the dragons. They must get away before anyone came upon them with swords. "Thank you," she said to the large dragon and dropped to a curtsy. It seemed the right thing to do.

The dragon bowed its head and little dragon made his funny sound. Then both dragons soared into the air and away in the other direction from the palace.

Poppy stared after them, hoping she would see them again one day. At least she had saved little dragon from the trap. She was almost at the bottom of the hill when her brother Percival, his friends, and some of the men came running toward her.

Percival stopped dead at the sight of her. Poppy put her hand up to her head. She had lost the hat while flying on the dragon's back and her hair was tumbled down her back.

"Poppy? What...? How...?" Percival stopped trying

to talk as he stared in disbelief.

As they walked back to the palace courtyard, the

other boys asked her questions, unable to believe

Poppy had ridden on the back of a fierce dragon.

"But how did you get on its back?" asked Alfred.

"Why did it not eat you?" asked Malcolm.

Percival seemed to have lost his voice and listened

in amazement as Poppy told her story about the trap.

She didn't care if no one believed her. It was the

most exciting adventure she might ever have.

Then Percival laughed and they all stopped

walking. "Ha, ha, that's a good story, Poppy. Did

you read that in one of your books? And why are you wearing my clothes and carrying my spare sword?"

Poppy looked at each of the boys in turn. Percival's words had made them all laugh. Then she remembered what she had in the bag at her belt. Untying the string, Poppy pulled out a piece of light green scale and held it up.

"Here's my proof, Percival. Some of little dragon's scales came off when its foot got caught in the trap. Would you like one for good luck? It might keep you safe from the bigger dragon."

While Percival stood with open mouth, his friends clamoured for a dragon scale. "Yes, please, Poppy!"

Me, please, Poppy!"

Poppy smiled. They believed her now. She looked

at her brother. He looked at her.

"Can I please have a dragon scale, Poppy? And

you can keep my spare sword," Percival said.

Poppy thought for a moment. If she was bored

one day in the future, she might borrow her brother's

clothes again and go on another adventure.

"You can have a dragon scale, Percival, but I

don't want your short sword. I'm going to find a

bigger one. But I'd like to keep your spare clothes in

case I have to ride on the dragon's back again." She

smiled at their expressions. "And don't worry. I'll

protect you all from its fire."

Poppy tossed back her golden curls and marched

back to the palace in front of the boys, feeling like

the bravest knight in the land.

the end.

A Royally Rotten Red Day

by Suzanne Purvis

Once there was a young Princess named Camelia

who lived in a very strange and colorful kingdom. It

looked like a normal, everyday kingdom, with castles,

and moats, and a dragon or two. But in this kingdom

the sun shone not only a glorious gold, it

shone many different colors. And the color of the sun

depended on the mood of the royal family.

Now most of the time, Princess Camelia and her

family were happy and the sun shone a bright, bold,

daffodil yellow. Of course, there had been a few

boring brown days. And there had been plenty of

plumy pink days. But today was different.

In the morning, when Princess Camelia slid from

under her royal quilt, the first thing she heard was,

POP. SNAP. CRACK. Her palace had crumbled. Not

the actual palace where she lived, but the one she

had just stepped on. The one that had taken her

three days and three hundred pieces to build. The one

that had been absolutely perfect.

"Oh no!" Princess Camelia cried. "How could this have happened? I'll never build it again so perfectly." She wanted to scream. She opened her mouth to let out a wail when she heard...

"Oh, Camelia darling. Please hurry and get dressed," her mother, the Queen said.

Princess Camelia snapped her mouth shut and growled.

And the sun shone a little less lemony.

Princess Camelia hurried to her cabinet of crowns and gowns. But when she opened the cabinet door, she found her pet dragon Darcy surrounded by smoke.

"Darcy! What are you doing?" she shrieked.

"I'm practicing my fire breathing. You know I

need a lot of practice," Darcy said, sputtering and coughing.

"Not in here," Princess Camelia cried. "Look at my gowns and crowns. They're sooty. And stinky. And singed." Princess Camelia clenched her fists. She wanted to scream. She opened her mouth to let out a wail when she heard...

"Camelia dear, breakfast," the Queen called.

Princess Camelia snapped her mouth shut and growled.

And the sun turned a fierce orange.

But that wasn't all. Princess Camelia's day got worse.

Prince Victor, her brother, had used her toothbrush

to polish his armor.

"Yuck!" Princess Camelia spit out the polish and paste, and chased after her brother. Running down the stairs, she found the palace peacocks scampering inside the castle. "Oops." Princess Camelia remembered she had been the last one to close the peacocks' gilded cage.

Then during her art lesson in the garden a flock of swans flew overhead. But the swans must have been molting because feathers rained down like snow and stuck everywhere. Feathers in her hair, feathers on her dress, and feathers glued to her almost perfect painting.

Princess Camelia ground her teeth together. She

wanted to scream. She opened her mouth to let out a wail when she heard...

"Camelia, it's time to go. We're launching the Royal Navy's newest ship," the Queen said.

Princess Camelia snapped her mouth shut and growled.

And the sun turned the darkest shade of orange.

Then the day got even worse.

Down on the royal docks, with the entire kingdom watching, Princess Camelia caused the most disastrous mishap. All she was supposed to do was lightly swing a bottle of bubbly juice at the bow of the ship. But because she'd had such a royally rotten day, she swung the bottle too hard.

SWOOSH. CRASH! SPLAT! The ship rocked,

causing a gigantic wave to splash over the docks.

Princess Camelia, the Queen, and most of the

kingdom stood drenched, dripping, and soaked.

Then Princess Camelia saw the Queen's face flush.

She saw the Queen's fists clench. She heard the

Queen's teeth grind. The Queen looked upset. And

she was. Because the Queen had not been having a

golden day either.

It had all started that morning when the Queen

had thrown open the brocade drapes and heard...

SMASH! CRASH! Her favorite potted plant had

fallen to the floor. "Not my blooming violets!"

the Queen cried. "It's taken me two years and two

different-sized pots to get these violets to grow and bloom." But then she heard...

"Mom, now what will I wear? Darcy, my dragon has singed all my clothes!"

When the Queen went to the royal dining room, she heard...

CRUNCH. MUNCH. YUM. Peacocks pecking at the family's breakfast.

Then the Queen heard...

"Mom, Victor used my toothbrush!"

But that wasn't all. The Queen's day got worse.

Swan feathers filled the garden and stuck to the royal feast that had been set up in honor of the ship launch.

The royal trumpeters all had colds and could not play at the ship launch.

And the King sent word. He was delayed on his journey. He would not be back for the ship launch.

Then at the ship launch, the day got even worse - Princess Camelia's disastrous mishap.

SWOOSH! CRASH! SPLAT! SPLASH!

Now both the Queen and the princess stood soaked and upset.

And the sun darkened to a deep fiery red.

"AHHHHHHHHHHHHHHHHHHHHH." The Princess and the Queen wailed. "What a royally rotten red day I've had," they both said.

Princess Camelia looked at the Queen. The Queen

looked at Princess Camelia. And the whole kingdom

looked up at the raging red sun, which was getting

hotter and hotter and redder and redder.

"We have to do something," the Queen cried.

"We're much too upset."

Suddenly, Princess Camelia had an idea. They had

to get rid of the swirling red in both their heads. "Do

you know how I feel?" Princess Camelia said. "I'm as

mad as a bull." So she stomped and snorted just like

a bull.

The Queen stared at her daughter. But she had to

agree, she was as angry as a bull too. So the Queen

stomped and snorted just like a bull.

And the blood red sun dimmed to crimson.

Princess Camelia pawed at the air. "I'm as mad as a bear," she said.

The Queen stared. But she had to agree she was as irked as a bear too. So she pawed the air.

And the sun cooled to a rusty maroon.

Princess Camelia said, "I'm as steamed as a snake." So she wiggled and hissed.

The Queen stared. But she had to agree she was as steamed as a snake too. So she wiggled and hissed.

And the sun cooled to orange.

Princess Camelia looked at her mother wiggling and hissing, and she couldn't help but giggle. And the Queen looked at Princess Camelia and she giggled too. Soon the whole kingdom was laughing as hard as a herd of hyenas.

And the sun transformed back to a gleaming glorious gold.

Everyone returned to the palace where they feasted in the garden, being careful to pick the feathers from their food. And when the King arrived, the royal family proclaimed a new family rule. When your mood turns bad, it's best to stomp, snort, wiggle or hiss – before the day turns royally rotten.

the end.

Blithe and Mirth: a Jolly Tale

by Kai Strand

"Father, do I really need to meet these princes?"

Blithe asked, slumping in her throne. "Haven't we met

enough

already?"

Perched in his larger throne next to Blithe, her

father wore a stormy expression as he examined her.

"Blithe Merry Jocund! How many times do we need

to go over this? You will find a prince to marry or I

will find him for you. Sit up straight."

With a dramatic sigh and a roll of her eyes,

Blithe pushed herself to the edge of her throne. She adjusted the golden circlet on her head, which was always falling askew. Someday she'd invent a crown that wouldn't tilt every time she climbed a tree or slid down a banister. Finally, she folded her hands in her lap like a proper princess.

The large double doors of the throne room swung open and the direst retinue Blithe had ever witnessed entered. They trudged into the room as if it were a knee-deep peat bog. They chanted what sounded like a funeral dirge as they step...pause...stepped into the room. Each and every one of them was cloaked in deep midnight blue that appeared almost black. Blithe gnawed her lower lip and stole a glance at her father.

She was relieved to see his brow furrowed.

Their prince stepped forward...and yawned.

Blithe's mouth fell agape. She peeked again at her father who glowered at the rude visitor.

A herald stepped forward and intoned in a dreary voice, "His Majesty, King of Frolicland, I present His Royal Highness," he took a deep breath, "Prince Haggard of Wearydom."

The prince yawned and gave a sleepy smile.

"Oh Father, no!" Blithe whispered.

"No, indeed," King Gambol agreed. He quickly dispatched the people of Wearydom and called for the next of the visitors to be presented.

This time when the doors swung open a more

normal entourage entered. They filed into the large

room at the usual pace, smiling to the gallery and

dropping into proper bows or curtsies when assembled

for the king and princess. All except for one man who

buzzed around the room measuring candlesticks and

doorframes and women's waists with a long ribbon.

He jotted notes, chewed his writing utensil, and

mumbled incessantly under his breath.

A herald stepped forward. "His Majesty, King

of Frolicland, I present His Royal Highness, Prince

Precise of Logicland."

Blithe scanned the entourage, waiting for the

prince to step forward.

"Prince Precise," the herald repeated, peering

nervously out the corner of his eye.

A squeal erupted from the gallery. The measuring man knelt in front of a woman, holding her foot in his hand, trying in vain to measure it. The woman attempted to yank her foot from his grasp while hitting him on the head with her fan.

"Sir!" the herald cried.

The man popped to his feet and spun to face the thrones. "Oh, pardon me! I do get distracted when there are new measurable items around."

He bustled to the front of the entourage and bowed deeply, letting his measuring tape unravel to the floor. He marked the measurement of his bow with a thumbnail. "An honor, sir."

King Gambol glared. "You are Prince Precise?"

"Yes, sire."

King Gambol glanced over to the woman in the gallery who'd collapsed into her seat in a faint. He dismissed the entourage from Logicland immediately.

"Thank you, Father," Blithe said, wiping her brow in relief. "May I go? I want to ride Sunshine out to the fields and pick some daisies."

"Yes, my dear you may..." but the entrance of a page carrying the standard of Vividom interrupted the king.

The young man was panting and coated with road dust. He dropped to a knee in front of the dais and bowed his head.

Blithe was struck by his clothing. Even under a layer of dirt she saw it was multiple colors and a jolly pattern. His hat held a jaunty feather and the toes of his shoes came to an amusing point.

"Speak," the king said to the bowed head.

"Sir, our party was delayed by bandits. No one was hurt, but we were not able to meet our appointment time. My prince requested that I come ahead to beg a delay in our presentation to your daughter."

The king considered the page. "When will your party arrive?"

"Before the evening's meal, sire. Actually, my prince would like to suggest a ball be held in Princess

Blithe's honor."

"That is rather forward of him," the king grumbled.

"He has also given instructions, sire."

"Instructions!" King Gambol bellowed. "The nerve."

"The prince will attend the ball in disguise. He would like Princess Blithe to guess his identity."

"B...b...b," the king blathered.

"Oh, how fun!" Blithe exclaimed. "It's like a game, Father. Oh, please let's do it."

"It's absurd," the king claimed. His cloudy expression cleared when he looked upon his daughter's brilliant smile. "Oh, very well."

Blithe took extra care to dress for the ball. She

wore her favorite gown made of yellow silk and embroidered with a colorful field of wildflowers all around the skirt. She pulled her long dark curls back and donned her favorite crown. Golden children, hand-and-hand ringed her head. Her green eyes sparked with excitement as she examined her appearance in the mirror. Satisfied, she headed downstairs to the ball.

She entered the large room and was immediately struck by the amount of color. The people from the visiting kingdom were dressed in satins and silks of topaz and ruby in velvets of azure and emerald. Their smiles were as bright as their attire, and the room was filled with laughter.

Blithe practically skipped over to the king, who

scowled at her exuberance. As she curtsied to her

father, she was approached by a man and asked to

dance. She appraised him as they twirled around

the room. Older and rather fond of birds, she didn't

imagine this man was a royal.

Her partner was replaced with another who had

impeccable manners and held himself very straight. He

smiled easily and wasn't bad to look at. This might

be the man. A jester approached and they stopped

dancing to watch him. The jester presented a coin for

all to see. He bit it to demonstrate its authenticity

and then handed it to Blithe for her examination. She

nodded gamely and handed the coin back to him. He

held it, passed a hand in front of it and suddenly it disappeared.

Blithe gasped and laughed.

He pointed to her green satin slipper.

"No," she breathed, but she slipped her shoe off and found the coin inside. Her heart burst with merriment. The man she'd been dancing with laughed and clapped. She handed the coin to the jester and thanked him, then continued her dance with the royal possibility.

She danced with all the men there. Her cheeks ached from smiling and her throat grew parched from laughter. One partner made up for his two left feet by sharing battle stories so enthralling, she frequently stopped dancing altogether to stare in awe at the imagined spectacle his words created. Certainly a prince was expected to be a brave knight as well.

Another partner regaled her with tales of his travels throughout Vividom. His love for the people of the country was apparent by the twinkle in his eye as he related his visits, meetings, and the occasional mishap.

Another man made her stomach growl with a recounting of his favorite meals. Decedent dishes such as pheasant in mushroom sauce with whipped lentil soup, herbed venison pastry with a raspberry lemon drizzle, or mutton and lentil stew in a crusty bread bowl. All meals fit for a king, or perhaps a prince?

All the while she was continually distracted by the jolly jester in his bright diamond patterned costume with jingling bells on his toes. As he worked his way through the crowd dancing, walking on his hands, or thrilling the people with magic, she often forgot to ask her dance partner questions that might help her determine his identity.

The end of the night drew near and the same young page who visited the throne room earlier in the day approached her with a bow. She was glad to see him because she thought her feet would fall off if she had to dance another dance.

"Princess Blithe, were you able to identify the

prince among us?" he asked.

Blithe looked out into the sea of smiling faces. Suddenly she wanted nothing more than to be right. She already loved these people and would be honored to become their princess. Her eyes found her second dance partner. The nice looking, well-mannered man most certainly could be the prince. She gnawed her lower lip and took a deep breath.

"I do not know if the man I am going to identify is of royal birth or not. I do know that he has been a source of joy for me this evening and that to me he is a prince." Blithe turned and scanned the crowd and finally spotted the funny three-pointed hat. "The jester is my prince tonight."

The crowd inhaled. The jester cocked his head.

As he walked toward her the people parted for him.

When he stood in front of her, he removed his hat

and bowed.

"Prince Mirth, Your Royal Highness."

Blithe drew in a breath. Her eyes sparked with

gaiety. "You truly are the prince?"

"Yes, I am."

"I almost picked him." Blithe pointed to her

second dance partner.

"You would not have been completely wrong. That

is my younger brother, Prince Sport."

Blithe examined Prince Mirth. He was the kind of

man who smiled with his eyes. "Sir, it is a pleasure

to meet you."

"The pleasure is mine." He held out his arm. "May

I have this dance?"

Suddenly her feet no longer ached and her spirit

soared like an eagle. She curtsied to the prince.

"Prince Mirth, you may have all my dances."

the end.

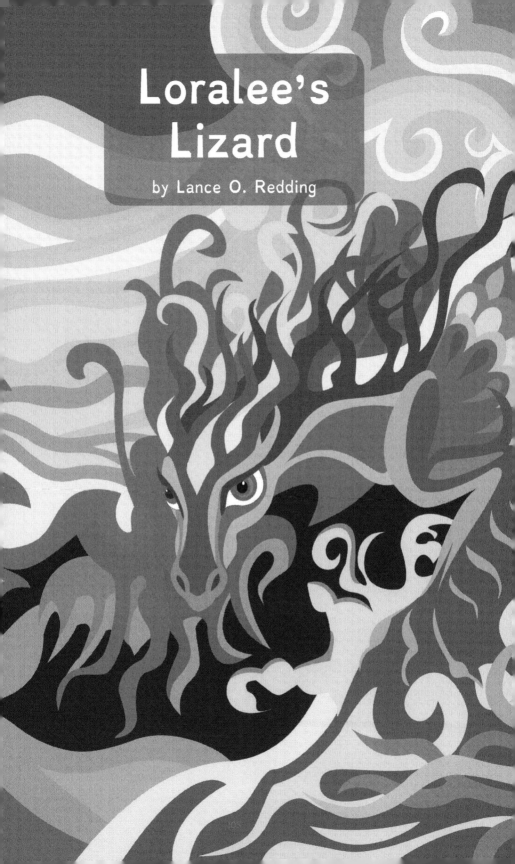

Loralee's
Lizard

by Lance O. Redding

Hi. My name is Loralee and I need to tell you something. Can you keep a secret? I hope so, because I don't have any other friends and there is no one else in my family or school I can trust. But I can't keep this inside any longer. I **HAVE** to tell **SOMEONE** or I'm going to explode! I think I might be going crazy, or something, so I need your help.

Okay, are you ready? I have a pet dragon. No, no, don't go away. I'm being totally one hundred and twenty-three percent serious. It's okay if you don't believe me. At first I didn't believe it, either. Just hear me out, though, and you'll see what I mean.

It all started a few weeks ago when I got a surprise package for my birthday. I have never gotten a birthday present before, but that's a whole

different story. Needless to say, I was super-duper

curious about what was inside, especially because

I didn't know who had sent the package. When

I reached into the box to pull out the present,

something poky and spiky squirmed and squiggled in

my hand, and out came what looked like a lizard. It

had brown, scaly skin, but the scales were big and

pointy and jutted out from its body. It wasn't pointy

enough to really hurt, but it's definitely not normal

lizard skin. I know this because I have seen a lot of

lizards. Since I don't have any friends, I go to the

pet store a lot. Animals don't think I'm weird, and as

far as I'm concerned, animals are a lot nicer than all

those mean kids at school.

Anyway, so there I was, all alone in the house with a brown lizard thing on my table when suddenly, she spoke to me! Not with her mouth, but, you know, inside my mind. It wasn't really words... it was more like pictures. And the first thing she told me was POTTY! (I guess she'd been in the box for a really long time). I took her into the back garden and let her do her business. When we came back inside we sat down and just sort of stared at each other.

That's when the second picture came into my mind. **BUGS!** Ew, I hate bugs. But I knew my new friend was hungry, so back outside we went to hunt some bugs. Unfortunately, I had to touch a couple of grasshoppers and some slimy earthworms, but all in all it wasn't too bad. At least I didn't have to deal with any nasty spiders!

Once we were back in the house things started getting weird.

"Hello," said the lizard. By this time I knew she wasn't a normal lizard and something in my mind kept repeating the word "dragon" over and over and over and over and... well, you get the idea.

"Um, hi," I said. "I'm Loralee. What's your name?" I kind of felt weird talking to a lizard, but since we had only just met I didn't know what else to say.

She sent a picture of a sword into my mind.

"Sword?" I asked, a little baffled. What a weird

name for a dragon.

She shook her head. Hmmm... what else could it be?

"Dagger?" Nope, wrong again. "Blade? Spike? Metal thingy? Long poky stick thing?" I tried about twenty other names but none of them were it. She was obviously getting frustrated toward the end because she kept biting my finger — not hard, mind you, but hard enough for me to know I was wrong.

"Can I just call you sword for now?" I finally suggested. She rolled her eyes, which I think meant okay, because she didn't bite me anymore.

Follow me, she sent.

I followed her out into the garden, grateful that

Mum wasn't home yet. She would have freaked out

if she saw a lizard in the house. So there we were,

in the garden for the third time in half an hour, when

my little lizard dragon thing looked up at me and her

black eyes sort of glossed over. She got this really

far away look in her eyes.

Touch me, she sent.

Weird, I thought. What's going on here? But I was

so curious about this animal who could talk to me

that I reached out and touched the tip of my finger

to one of the scales on her back.

That's when I started falling.

I hit the ground but it didn't hurt, and at the same

time a loud bang sounded in my ears. It was still

ringing as I opened my eyes and looked around to see what had happened. Immediately I knew I wasn't in my garden anymore. I didn't know where I was, but I was fairly certain we weren't even on Earth because I could see two suns blazing in the sky.

It looked like we were in some kind of forest. The trees were tall and dark green. Very little light made it all the way down to the forest floor because there were just so many trees. I stood up, wiped the dust off my knees, and turned in a circle. Where was I? How was I ever going to get home? Panic welled up inside me, pushing up past my beating heart, past my voice box that wanted to scream (but I was too scared to do that cause who knows what kind of beasties lived in this forest) and all the way up to my

eyeballs where tears started to form.

That's when I saw her. Sword, my dragon. This

time it was easy to see she really was a dragon

because she was about a million times bigger and she

had beautiful swirly colors all over her body. Oh, and

she had wings that sparkled in the sunlight. That was

a big clue.

She saw my tears and sent, it's okay. Don't worry,

I'm here to protect you. A sense of peace settled

over me, and I realized I could understand her here —

not just pictures and images in my head, but actual

words!

"Hey, I can understand you here!" I said.

Yes, she sent.

"Coooool."

Come.

She only said the one word, but along with that

I saw an image of me flying on her back. Now things

were getting exciting! Of course, I was a little bit

nervous deep down inside but at the same time I still

felt calm, like everything was going to be okay. I

knew I could trust Sword.

Stop calling me Sword, she sent.

"Well, what's your name then?" I asked.

Razor, she sent.

"Razor? A girl dragon named Razor? Weird. Can I

call you Razy instead? Or maybe just Raze? Oooh, I

know, how about Raz?"

She laughed as I climbed on her back. It was a clear-as-crystal, pure-as-spring-water sound and it filled me up with bubbles of laughter inside. I could feel everything my dragon felt, like we were connected at the hip, or brain, maybe. Or better yet, we were connected at the heart.

That's when I felt the sadness. Somewhere deep down inside Raz there was a dark pool of sadness.

"What's wrong?" I asked.

Come, she sent again. So I climbed up on her back and off we went.

Now, I have to tell you that flying is absolutely amazing — probably the most awesomest thing I've ever experienced in my whole life — but right at that moment I couldn't pay attention to how cool it was because of two things.

First, it was super-duper cold and flying through the air only made it colder. Plus, the farther we went, the colder it got! Pretty soon we were flying over land covered in snow, heading high up into a mountain. My teeth chattered uncontrollably. I couldn't take this much longer!

The second reason I couldn't pay attention to flying was because the pool of sadness inside Raz grew bigger and bigger the farther we flew. Something was wrong and wherever we were going, it made her think more and more about it.

Finally we landed in a small cave in the middle of the large mountain. It was big enough for Raz to fly straight into and land. I was so frozen that Raz had to crouch down super low so I could sort of slide off, like a pile of frozen ice cream falling onto the floor. She blew fire up at the ceiling, which radiated heat through the whole cave and warmed me up in just under two minutes flat.

Then she walked toward the back of the cave and pointed at a pile of rocks.

There, she sent. My baby. Please help.

I looked closer and what I first thought was a round rock on top of all the others was actually an egg. A dragon egg!

"What's wrong?" I asked.

She's not hatching, Raz sent. It's too cold. The weather has changed. She needs sand, not rocks. She sent me a picture of a warm beach with the sun shining down on an egg half-buried in the sand.

"Hmmmm" I said. I was stumped. I had never even been to a beach. But then I remembered a lesson from school from two years ago. Yeah, I'm kind of a geek that way. I remember stuff. That's one of the reason other kids don't like me very much.

"I know of a beach we could take her," I said. "Turtle Island Beach! I remember exactly what it looks like. Let's go there right away!"

Razor smiled a big dragon smile, which would have

been super scary if I hadn't felt how happy she was

on the inside, because on the outside all I could see

were big dragon teeth that looked like they were

ready to gobble me up in one big gulp!

Going to the island was a bit harder than I

thought it would be, though. Raz couldn't just

transport all three of us while we stood there. I had

to lift up her baby egg, and man, that thing was

heavy! I'm talking, like, five bowling balls. Or maybe

a hundred! I lifted the egg and she got down really

low, again. It was hard work, but I finally managed to

climb on top.

"Do we have to fly through all the cold air

again?" I asked.

No, she sent. Just think of a picture of the island

and we'll go straight there.

I imagined the picture from the text book. The

island was famous for how pristine it was. It had

only been discovered a couple of years ago and was

too hard for most people to get to — even with

boats and airplanes. The picture in the book was so

beautiful I had stared at it for a whole week in class.

I had dreamed about running away and living on the

island. A perfect paradise! And that meant it was

the perfect place to hide a dragon egg. It had to

work. Besides, it was the only beach picture I'd ever

looked at, so it was the only choice we had.

"I've got the picture in my head," I said. The

falling sensation came again. Transporting sure is weird. I held on tight to the egg, and when the loud banging noise sounded I scrambled to my feet and looked around, worried someone else might be there. We couldn't risk anyone else seeing us.

The beach was beautiful and warm, and most importantly, empty. Still, we took our time and found a nice hidden spot, just in case there were visitors. We went back and forth between my house and the island every day to check on the egg, and after a week I was used to the falling sensation of transporting. I also had a nice pair of earmuffs to cancel out the loud banging noise.

We would sneak away during lunch at school —

nobody ever noticed I was gone — and I would eat and talk with Raz on the warm sand of Turtle Island Beach. After a month we saw the first crack in the egg. The next day there were three more. Raz, of course, stayed with the egg every day from then on and only came to get me during lunch time.

I was there when it happened — when the baby dragon finally came out of its shell. You're probably thinking, oh, how sweet! Well, it really wasn't cause it was all gooey and slimy and honestly, it looked really weird. But I could feel love filling Raz up to the very tippy top of her wings, and it helped me a lot. Otherwise I probably would have run away I was so grossed out.

Raz began a beautiful crooning song, and the baby

dragon walked over to her. She licked the goo off,

and the baby's scales shone and glistened in the sun.

Its wings were so small and weak it couldn't open

them yet, but they were the prettiest part on the

baby — see-through and pearly and glossy, all at the

same time, like a beautiful wet jewel shining in the

sunlight.

The baby dragon looked up at me and smiled. I

decided it looked much better now that all the gunk

was off. I reached out and patted it on the head. It

crooned along with Raz, and the three of us just sat

there and enjoyed the moment. That was last night.

After that, we all went home to my house so we

could stay together.

Raz and her baby are wrapped up now in my underwear drawer. I figure that's the safest place in my room. Mum never looks in there — she makes me do all my own laundry.

It's morning now and I woke up feeling better than I've felt in a long time. Not only do I have two amazing new friends and lots of adventures sure to come, but I have a secret that no one else knows! Well, except for you. But you'll keep my secret, right? After all, that's what best friends do.

the end.

Register:

Register on our website (www.knowonder.com/register) to get **FREE** access to over 500 orignal stories, education tools and other resources to help you give the gift of literacy to your child, each and every day.

About Us:

Knowonder is a leading publisher of engaging, daily content that drives literacy; the most important factor in a child's success.

Parents and educators use Knowonder tools and content to promote reading, creativity, and thinking skills in children from zero to twelve.

Knowonder's Literacy Program - delivered through storybook collections - delivers original, compelling new stories every day, creating an opportunity for parents to connect to their children in ways that significantly improve their children's success.

Ultimately, Knowonder's mission is to eradicate illiteracy and improve education success through content that is affordable, accessible, and effective.

Learn more at

www.knowonder.com

18334729R00071

Printed in Great Britain
by Amazon